SPELLING BEE

Look for these
and other books
in
The Kids in Ms. Colman's Class series

2 A

STONEYBROOK
ACADEMY

Jannie, Bobby, Tammy, Sara
Ian, Leslie, Hank, Terri, Pamela
Nancy, Omar, Audrey, Chris, Ms. Colman
Karen, Hannie, Ricky, Natalie

THE KIDS IN MS. COLMAN'S CLASS

SPELLING BEE

Ann M. Martin

Illustrations by Charles Tang

A
LITTLE APPLE
PAPERBACK

SCHOLASTIC INC.
New York Toronto London Auckland Sydney

ISBN 0-590-06005-8

12 11 10 9 8 7 6 5 4 3 2 1   8 9/9 0 1/0 2/0

Printed in the U.S.A.   40
First Scholastic printing, January 1998

This book is for
Brett, Katelyn, and Jenna Godwin

HANK REUBENS

Hank Reubens lay in his bed. His cat, Patch, was sleeping on his feet. His dog, Jack, was sleeping on the floor by the bed. Hank yawned. He loved the early morning when it was still dark outside and no one else in his family was awake.

Hank tried to guess what time it was. Ten minutes to six, he thought. He rolled over and looked at his clock. That was close. It was fifteen minutes to six.

Excellent, thought Hank. He would be able to play on his computer before it was time to get ready for school. Hank turned on his light. Patch blinked at him from the end of the bed. Jack thumped his tail,

1

but he did not even bother to open his eyes.

Nobody else in Hank's family liked getting up early. Except for Hank's mother, but Hank's mother lived in Florida now. That was a long way from Stoneybrook, Connecticut. Stoneybrook was where Hank and his sisters and his father lived. (And, of course, Patch and Jack.) But not Mrs. Reubens. She and Hank's father had gotten divorced, and she had moved to Florida. Hank missed her, even though he and his sisters visited pretty often. Sometimes they spent vacations in Winter Park with their mother. Hank had been to Walt Disney World two times so far.

Hank's sisters were twins. They were five years old. Polly and Susan could be pests, but Hank found that he liked them better now that they were in kindergarten. Hank and Polly and Susan went to Stoney-brook Academy. Hank was in the second grade. His teacher was Ms. Colman, and she was Hank's all-time favorite teacher.

(She was the favorite teacher of just about every kid in the class.)

Hank put on his slippers. He sat at his desk. He turned on his computer. Hank had lots of good software for his computer — mostly games and puzzles. Hank liked solving problems of any kind. He liked math puzzles, word puzzles, and brain-busters. He was even pretty good at solving mysteries. He thought he might be either a professor or a detective when he grew up.

Hank had just started working on a very hard word puzzle when he heard a soft knock at his door. Then Polly poked her head in the room.

"What are you doing up?" Hank asked her.

"Susan is snoring," Polly replied. "Can I help you?"

"I don't think so. I am solving a puzzle. And you have to know how to spell to solve this puzzle," said Hank.

"I know how to spell. P-O-L-L-Y. That is my name. H-O-R-S. Horse."

"E," said Hank.

"Horsie?"

"No. Add an E at the end."

"Oh. How about X-R-L-A-P?"

"What is that?" asked Hank.

"Don't *you* know?" said Polly.

Hank shrugged.

Polly was not a very good speller. Yet. But Hank was. He was one of the best in his class. He was good at math too. In fact, he was good at just about everything in school.

Hank let Polly sit in his lap. He showed her how to play the game. Then he started a mystery puzzle. Hank had just ten minutes in which to figure out who had robbed a jewelry store. Was it the tall woman in the red coat? The man in the checkered —

"Hank!" called his father. "Time to get ready for school. You too, Polly."

"Okay." Hank turned off his computer. He could solve the puzzle later. Now it was time for another day in Ms. Colman's class.

MORNING IN ROOM 2A

Mr. Reubens dropped Hank and his sisters off in front of Stoneybrook Academy. Hank walked Polly and Susan inside. He took them to their kindergarten class. Then he walked down the hall to the door that said 2A.

Ms. Colman's class.

Hank stepped inside. He looked at the room. Ms. Colman's desk was in the front. The chalkboard was behind her desk. In front of her desk were four rows of smaller desks. A row of four, a row of five, and two more rows of four. Seventeen kids were in Hank's class. And eight of them were there now. Ms. Colman had not arrived yet. But the door to Mr. Berger's room was open and Hank knew Mr. Berger was keeping an eye on everyone until Ms. Colman arrived.

Mr. Berger was the other second-grade teacher. His classroom was next door. An inside doorway joined the two rooms. Hank liked being able to go into Mr. Berger's room without going into the hallway. It was like a secret door in the game of Clue.

"Hi, Hank!" called Ian Johnson.

Ian was standing by a large cage. He was holding Hootie. Hootie was the guinea pig that belonged to the kids in 2A.

"Hi!" Hank called back. Hank went to the coatroom. He took off his ski jacket and snow pants and hat and mittens and boots. He put his lunch in his cubby. Then he took a book of brainteasers out of his cubby. He carried it to his desk. Hank sat in the very last row. The rest of the kids in his row were girls. That was not surprising. There were eleven girls in Ms. Colman's room and only six boys. Besides Hank and Ian,

the boys were Ricky Torres, Omar Harris, Bobby Gianelli, and Chris Lamar. Those four were very good friends. They were a tight bunch. Sometimes they let Hank and Ian play with them; sometimes they did not. Sometimes they were nice to Hank and Ian; sometimes they were not.

Hank sat at his desk. He opened his book of brainteasers. He found a new brainteaser. It was about the animals in a barn, and how many eggs six roosters could lay. While Hank thought about the problem, he looked around the room. He saw Karen Brewer, Hannie Papadakis, and Nancy Dawes scurry to a corner of the room. Those girls were always together. They called themselves the Three Musketeers. Karen was bossy and a smarty-pants. Hank was glad she sat in the first row (right in front of Ms. Colman, where their teacher could keep an eye on her). However, Nancy and Hannie sat next to Hank in the back row. The fourth person in the back row was Jannie Gilbert, who did not like the Three Musketeers very much. Jannie and her two best friends, Pamela Harding and Leslie Morris, were the Three Musketeers' best enemies.

Hank watched Bobby and Omar run around the room with a football. Then the twins arrived. The twins were Tammy and Terri Barkan, who were sometimes hard to tell apart. Next came Audrey Green and Sara Ford, more best friends, and then Chris and Ricky. The last person to arrive was Natalie Springer. Natalie sat in the front row with Karen and Ricky Torres. The three of them wore glasses, just like Ms. Colman did. Ms. Colman liked people with glasses to sit near the chalkboard. (The fourth person in the front row was Bobby, who did not wear glasses. Hank had a feeling Ms. Colman liked to keep her eye on Bobby as well as on Karen.)

"Hey, Hank! Come here!" Bobby called then. "Want to play monkey-in-the-middle with Omar and me?"

"No thanks," Hank replied. He had a pretty good idea who the monkey would be. Hank went back to his book. And right away he solved the brainteaser. The answer was zero. *No* eggs would be laid, because roosters do not lay eggs, chickens do.

3

THE STAR CLUB

"Good morning, girls and boys!"

Hank looked up from his book. Ms. Colman had arrived. His classmates ran for their seats. Ms. Colman set her things on her desk. She hung her coat in the coatroom. She called hello to Mr. Berger. Then, quietly, she closed the door to his room.

Ms. Colman began the day. She asked Chris to take attendance. She reminded the kids to bring in their lunch money. She reminded Natalie that she needed to hand in a math worksheet. And then she said, "Class, I have an announcement to make."

The kids wiggled in their seats. Ms.

11

Colman's announcements were usually good. Or at least interesting.

"A new club is starting here at Stoney-brook Academy," said Ms. Colman. "It will be called the Star Club. Several students from each class have been chosen to be part of the club. The club will meet in the library one afternoon each week for two months. And the kids in the club will get to work on special activities and projects, and go on field trips."

At this, Hank saw Chris lean forward and poke Bobby in the back. Bobby turned around (quickly, so Ms. Colman would not see him) and gave Chris a knowing look.

"The students in this class who have been chosen for the Star Club are Nancy Dawes, Sara Ford, Karen Brewer, and Hank Reubens. Congratulations to you," said Ms. Colman. "I will tell you more about the club later. Now, class, please take out your reading worksheets."

Hank rummaged in his desk. He did not look at his classmates. He wanted to groan. First of all, he was the only boy in 2A chosen for the new club. Hank and three girls. Hank did not mind the girls. Not at all. But he knew what the boys would say. (Well, not Ian. Ian would not care. But Omar, Ricky, Bobby, and Chris would.) Second, Hank already knew — and he knew that every other kid in the class already knew — that there was more to the Star Club than Ms. Colman had said. The Star Club, Hank was sure, was for smart kids. And he had an idea what Omar, Ricky, Bobby, and Chris would have to say about *that*.

The boys did not have a chance to say anything for awhile, though. Ms. Colman kept her class busy that morning. The kids read a story together, learned about lizards, cut a make-believe pizza into slices of different sizes, and finally chose books from the classroom library for reading time.

When everyone was settled quietly at their desks, Ms. Colman gathered Hank, Sara, Karen, and Nancy in the back of the room. They sat around a small table.

"I want to tell you more about the Star Club," Ms. Colman began. "I think you will enjoy being part of it. You will get to work on special projects, projects that will tickle your brains." She smiled at Hank. "The four of you learn our classwork easily. The Star Club will give you challenges that you do not always find in our classroom. I think you will enjoy the trips too."

"How many kids are in the club?" Sara wanted to know.

"About fifty," Ms. Colman replied. "But you will not meet with all of them. The first- and second-graders will be in your part of the club. Sixteen kids. You four, four from Mr. Berger's room, and four from each of the first-grade classes. Your first meeting will be on Wednesday, in two days. You will go to the library after recess and stay until the end of the day. Your Star Club teacher will be Mrs. Ellis."

Hank nodded. He knew, he just *knew*, what the other boys were going to say about the Star Club. And yet . . . Hank could not help feeling a teeny bit excited.

BRAINBUSTERS

"Hey, Smart Club!" called Ricky Torres.

Hank looked over his shoulder. He was standing on the playground with Karen, Nancy, and Sara. In ten minutes they would go to the library for their first meeting of the Star Club. They were wondering what kinds of things they would do. Nancy had said that she felt nervous.

And then Ricky had called to the kids.

Hank glared at Ricky. "It is not the *Smart* Club, it is the *Star* Club," he said crossly. "I keep telling you."

"Well, only smarties are in it," Ricky replied. "What is wrong with the rest of us? Are we too dumb for your club?"

"Ask the principal," said Sara. "Mrs. Titus is the one who decided who would be in the club."

Ricky made a face. He was about to say something else when the bell rang. Hank and the girls looked for Mrs. Ellis. They were going to walk inside with her and go straight to the library.

"Have fun, you smarties!" called Ricky.

Hank ignored him. He and Karen, Sara, and Nancy found Mrs. Ellis. She was standing with Edwin Grant, Debbie Dvorak, Mia Waters, and Oliver Chang from Mr. Berger's room.

"Hi, kids," she said. "Some of you already know me, and some of you do not. I am Mrs. Ellis and I teach science to the fifth- and sixth-graders. Let's hurry to the library now. The first-graders are waiting there with one of the library aides. I will tell you more about the Star Club when we have settled down."

Mrs. Ellis led the kids to the library. The second-graders took off their coats and boots and mittens. They sat at a long table with Mrs. Ellis and eight scared-looking first-graders.

Mrs. Ellis smiled. "Welcome to the Star Club," she said.

Hank relaxed. He could see some of the other kids relax too.

"The first thing to know about the Star Club," said Mrs. Ellis, "is that mostly you are going to have fun."

Mrs. Ellis told the kids about some of the projects and activities they would be working on. Then she handed out gold name tags shaped like stars. And then she set a large carton on the table. Across the top of the carton was written BRAINBUSTERS.

Hank grinned. Excellent, he thought.

"Today," said Mrs. Ellis, "we are going to get to know each other better with a brainbuster race."

Even more excellent, thought Hank.

The kids spent the rest of the after-

noon solving problems and puzzles. Sometimes they worked alone; sometimes they
worked together. Five boys and eleven girls
were Star Club members. But Hank did not
care who he worked with. He just liked
solving puzzles. And solving puzzles with
other kids who liked solving puzzles was
even better.

Just before the last bell rang, Mrs. Ellis
walked the kids back to their classrooms.

"How was the *Smart* Club?" Bobby

whispered as Hank passed his desk.

"Great," Hank replied. "Too bad you cannot join."

Later, as the kids in Ms. Colman's class were putting on their coats, Chris poked Hank in the side. "I passed by the library this afternoon," he said. "The Smart Club is a bunch of girls. I guess you are a girl too then, Hank."

"What is wrong with being a girl?" Hank replied. "The girls are much nicer than you guys are. *They* do not tease me or call me names."

Chris opened his mouth. Then he closed it. He did not know what to say to that. So he said nothing at all.

5

KAREN BREWER

One day Ms. Colman stood in front of her classroom. She was smiling. "Girls and boys," she said, "I have some news. Do you remember the spelling bees last fall?"

"Yes," said some of Hank's classmates. And Hank nodded his head. Of course he remembered them. First, a spelling bee had been held in their classroom. (A spelling bee had been held in every classroom at Stoneybrook Academy that day.) Karen Brewer had won that bee. And Hank had done well in it. For awhile he and Karen and Nancy were the only ones spelling words. Everyone else had missed a word already, and had had to sit down. Then Ms.

Colman had given Hank the word *alligator.* Hank had hesitated. "A-L," he had said. Then he almost said "I," but instead he said "*L*-I-G-A-T-" He paused. "E-R."

"Wrong!" Karen had cried. "It is *O*-R, not E-R." Karen had a big mouth. Kind of like an alligator. Which was probably why she had spelled the word right. Anyway, Karen had finally won the spelling bee. Then she had won another spelling bee when she was playing against the winners in the first, second, and third grades. That made her the junior champion at Stoneybrook Academy. After that, she had won *another* bee when she played against winners from other schools. (Finally she lost, but she did a lot of winning first.)

"Well," Ms. Colman went on, "we are going to have some more spelling bees. But just here at Stoneybrook Academy. The winners will not go on to play against students in other schools. This is what is going to happen. First we will have some practice spelling bees in our classroom. After awhile we will have a real spelling bee. At the same time, every other class will also have a spelling bee. The winner of our bee will have a 'spell-off' with the other second-grade winner — with the winner from Mr. Berger's room. We will have a spelling champ in each grade in our school."

"Cool," said Audrey.

"Excellent," said Ian.

"Yes," said Ms. Colman. "Cool and excellent. Just remember, though, that the spelling bees — the practice bees and the real ones — are mostly for fun. Fun with spelling. Okay, kids?"

Hank thought about what Ms. Colman had said. And then he forgot about the spelling bees. He forgot about them entirely, until recess. Lunch was over, and the kids in Ms. Colman's class had run onto the playground. Hank and Ian were trying to decide what to do first when they heard a loud voice nearby. It belonged to Karen

Brewer. (Alligator Mouth, thought Hank.)

"Attention! Attention!" called Karen.

Most of the kids in 2A turned to look at her.

"I have an announcement," said Karen.

"No, *we* have an announcement," said Hannie Papadakis. Hannie, Nancy, Audrey, and Sara were standing next to Karen.

"Okay, *we* do," said Karen.

"So what is your big announcement?" asked Chris.

"A *girl* is going to win our class spelling bee," replied Karen.

"No, *Karen* is going to win it," said Audrey.

By now everyone was looking at Karen. And all the girls were crowded behind her.

"Girls are smarter than boys!" shouted Pamela.

"Girls rule!" cried Jannie.

"You girls just have big mouths," said Bobby.

"Yeah," agreed Ricky. "If you are so smart, tell us who is going to win the spelling bee in Mr. Berger's room."

"The same person who won last fall," said Nancy Dawes. "Debbie Dvorak."

"A *girl*," Pamela pointed out.

"Big deal," muttered Bobby.

The boys drifted away from the girls.

6

Boys Rule!

The first practice spelling bee was held after recess one day. Hank could tell that the girls could not wait for it to begin. He could hear several of them saying, "Girls rule, girls rule" under their breath. A very, very quiet chant.

"This is the way the practice spelling bee and all of the spelling bees will work," said Ms. Colman. "You will line up at the front of the classroom." (Ms. Colman pointed to the chalkboard.) "I will give a word to the first person in line. That person will repeat the word, spell it, then repeat it again. If he or she has spelled the word correctly, he or she will move to the end of the line. If the person has made a mistake, he or she must sit down. The last person left standing will be the winner after he or she has spelled the missed word correctly. Okay, class, please line up."

The kids in Ms. Colman's room ran to the chalkboard. The girls made sure they were first in line, with the boys at the end.

"We will begin with easy words," said Ms. Colman. She turned to Nancy, the first person in line. "Desk," said Ms. Colman.

"Desk," repeated Nancy. "D-E-S-K. Desk."

"Very good," said Ms. Colman. "You are still in the game. You may move to the end of the line."

The next person in line was Hannie. "Take," Ms. Colman said to her.

"Take. T-A-K-E. Take," said Hannie.

"Very good," said Ms. Colman again.

The spelling bee continued. For a long time, the kids spelled every word correctly. No one had to sit down. Then Ms. Colman said to Chris, "Pencil."

"Pencil," repeated Chris. "P-E-N-S-I-L. Pencil."

"I am sorry. That is incorrect," said Ms. Colman. "Chris, please take your seat. Chris's word goes to the next person in line. Nancy?"

"Pencil," said Nancy. "P-E-N-C-I-L. Pencil."

"Yes!" cried Karen and a couple of other girls.

And Hank heard the twins chanting, "Girls rule, girls rule."

The words in the spelling bee grew

harder. More and more kids left the line and returned to their seats. Finally only Hank and Karen were left in the line.

"Mirror," Ms. Colman said to Hank.

Hank paused. He pictured a mirror. He thought for a moment. At last he said, "Mirror. M-I-R-O-R. Mirror."

"I am sorry," said Ms. Colman. "That is incorrect. But do not sit down yet, Hank. If Karen cannot spell 'mirror' either, then I will give both of you another word."

"I can spell it," said Karen. She stood up straight. "Mirror. M-I-R-R-O-R. Mirror."

"Excellent!" exclaimed Ms. Colman. "Karen is the winner of our first practice spelling bee. And Hank, you came in second place. Good for you."

Nobody heard what Ms. Colman said to Hank, though. The girls drowned out her words. They were jumping up and down, shouting, "Girls rule, girls rule, girls rule!"

Two days later, Ms. Colman held the next practice spelling bee. Once again her students lined up in front of the chalk-board. Once again, the first words in the bee were easy. Then they became harder. And once again, after a long time, Karen and Hank were the only spellers left. When Karen misspelled "holiday," Hank spelled it correctly.

The girls were quiet. So were the boys. They stared at Hank. He was the winner.

The following week, a third spelling bee was held. Hank won that one too. And before he knew it, the boys in 2A were jumping up and down, shouting, "Boys rule, boys rule!"

FRIENDS

On the playground the next day, Ricky, Omar, Bobby, Chris, and Ian crowded around Hank.

"We will show the girls!" cried Omar.

"Yeah. 'Girls rule.' How stupid," said Bobby.

"*Boys* rule!" exclaimed Ricky.

Hank looked across the playground. Some of the girls were gathered by the swings. The rest of them stood in a group near the monkey bars. They were very quiet.

"You know what, Hank?" said Ricky.

"What," said Hank. He was pretty sure Ricky was going to say something about the Smart Club. Or that the boys did not really rule, since Hank was, in fact, a girl.

But instead Ricky said, "I think *you* are going to win the big spelling bee in our class, Hank. You are going to beat Karen. And *then* you are going to beat the winner in two-B. You will be the winner for the whole second grade."

"Yeah. A boy," said Omar. "The winner will be a boy."

"Want to play kickball with us?" Chris asked Hank.

"Oh," said Hank. "I don't know."

Hank was a pretty good kickball player. But sometimes the other boys, especially Bobby and Ricky, made him nervous.

"Well . . . what do *you* want to do?" Omar asked Hank.

Hank looked at Ian. "I was . . . um, I was going to study spelling words."

"I was going to help him," said Ian.

"Oh. Maybe that is a good idea," said Ricky.

Ricky, Bobby, Chris, and Omar walked away from Hank and Ian.

"Good luck!" Omar called over his shoulder.

That Friday, Ms. Colman said, "Class, we will have two more practice spelling bees next week, one on Monday and one on Wednesday. On Friday we will have our big spelling bee. All the other classes will hold their spelling bees on Friday too. So study your words. There is just one week until the big bee!"

Omar turned around in his seat. "The big bee that *you* are going to win, Hank," he said.

On the playground that day, Hank and Ian sat together on the steps by the cafeteria. Ian was going to help Hank study again.

"You need any help?" Ricky called from the monkey bars.

"That's okay!" Hank called back. "Thanks."

On Saturday, Hank was sitting in front of his computer. Outside his bedroom windows snow was falling. Hank heard the doorbell ring.

"Hank!" called his father from downstairs. "Some of your friends are here!"

Some of his friends? Hank was surprised. Ian came over every now and then, but that was about it. Who could be at the door?

Hank turned off his computer. He ran downstairs. Standing in the hallway were Bobby, Omar, and Ricky.

"Hi," said Hank. He did not know what else to say.

"Hi!" replied Bobby. He was grinning.

"I guess you are wondering why we are here," said Omar.

"Well . . . yeah," said Hank.

"We brought you some word lists," spoke up Ricky.

The boys held out some papers to Hank.

"We found them in the library," said Omar.

"The public library," added Ricky.

"They are spelling lists for all different grades. They go up to *fifth* grade," said Omar. "We think you can even spell fifth-grade words."

"And we are here to help you study," said Bobby.

Hank could not believe his luck. The boys wanted to help him. More importantly, they were not teasing him.

Boys Versus Girls

Hank studied the word lists with Omar, Ricky, and Bobby on Saturday. He studied them with Ian on Sunday. On Monday, the next practice spelling bee was held.

And the kids in Ms. Colman's class had a surprise. Jannie Gilbert had been studying spelling lists too. In the other spelling bees, Jannie was always one of the first kids to sit down. This time Jannie kept spelling her words correctly. Finally, Jannie, Karen, and Hank were the only kids left in line.

"Girls rule!" someone whispered loudly.

But Jannie missed the next word and had to sit down.

Then Karen missed the next word. "Bullfrogs," she muttered.

"Hank, try Karen's word, please," said Ms. Colman.

"Grateful," said Hank. "G-R-A-T-E-F-U-L. Grateful."

"Excellent!" exclaimed Ms. Colman. "Hank is our winner again."

"Yes!" said Bobby.

Omar shot up out of his seat. "Boys rule!" he cried.

"Okay, settle down now," said Ms. Colman. But she was smiling.

The next practice bee took place on Wednesday morning, just before lunch. One by one, the kids dropped out of the line until Hank and Karen were left. And Hank won again.

When he did, the boys began to cheer. At the same time, Hank could hear cheering in Mr. Berger's room.

At lunchtime that day, Hank said to Ian, "I wonder who has been winning the spelling bees in Mr. Berger's room."

Before Ian could answer, Chris, Bobby, Omar, and Ricky plopped down at their table. They opened their lunches.

"Debbie Dvorak has won some of the bees," said Chris, "and Edwin Grant has won some of them."

Omar unwrapped his sandwich. "All of the girls say Debbie is going to win the bee on Friday and all of the boys say Edwin is going to win."

"And all the girls in our class *still* think Karen is going to win," said Ricky. "But we boys know you are going to win, Hank."

Hank looked around the cafeteria. Debbie and the girls from 2B were sitting at one table. Edwin and the boys were at another table. Karen and the girls from 2A were at a third table. And then there were Hank and the boys from 2A.

"Boys versus girls," said Hank.

"And you are going to beat Karen," said Chris.

"Boys rule!" cried Bobby.

After lunch the second-grade boys stood together in a big bunch on the playground. The second-grade girls stood together in a bigger bunch not far from the boys. The boys looked at the girls. The girls looked at the boys. For a long time nobody said anything. Then Pamela Harding stuck her tongue out. She stuck it out just a little

bit — just the tip of her tongue. But Ricky saw her.

"I saw that, Pamela, you dumb girl!"

"I am not dumb!" replied Pamela.

"All girls are dumb," said Chris. "That is why you keep losing the spelling bees."

"Then how come *Debbie* wins some of *our* bees?" asked Mia Waters. "I guess it is because you boys are dumb."

"Kids? What is going on?" called Ms. Colman from across the playground.

"Nothing," replied most of the kids.

The boys and the girls drifted apart.

When the bell rang, Hank left his friends. It was time to line up for the Star Club. As he turned away, Ricky gave him a high five.

THE SPELLING BEE

"Hank! High five!"

"Hey, Hank! Boys rule!"

Hank smiled as he walked into room 2A. It was the day of the real and true spelling bee, and the boys were being VERY nice to him. So Hank smiled as he took off his coat. But inside he felt nervous. He could feel butterflies in his stomach. He felt jumpy and trembly. What if he lost the spelling bee? What would the boys think of him then? They had been *so* nice to Hank lately. But Hank knew that was only because the boys thought he was going to win and then they could say "Boys rule" and really mean it. What would they say if

Hank lost? Hank did not like to think about it. But he could not help thinking about it. He thought about it all morning and all during lunch and all during recess. After recess Ms. Colman said, "Okay, class, it is time for our spelling bee."

Hank's stomach turned over. He wished he had eaten a smaller lunch.

"Go, Hank!" Omar whispered, turning around in his seat.

"Please line up by the chalkboard," said Ms. Colman.

Once again the kids in Ms. Colman's class formed a line.

The spelling bee began.

Tammy was the first to make a mistake and sit down. Ricky was next. Soon Hank and Karen were the only kids standing at the front of the room.

Ms. Colman smiled at them. "Okay, you two. You know the rules," she said. "To win, one of you must spell a word correctly that the other has missed. If you

46

both miss a word, the game continues. Okay, Hank, you are next. Your word is 'believe.' "

"Believe," said Hank. "B-E-L-I-E-V-E. Believe."

"Very good," said Ms. Colman. "Karen? Calendar."

"Calendar," said Karen. "C-A-L-E-N-D-A-R. Calendar."

"Excellent."

For five more minutes Ms. Colman gave Hank and Karen words to spell. They did not make a mistake. Not until Ms. Colman said, "Okay, Hank. Gallery."

"Gallery. G-A-L-E-R-Y. Gallery."

"I am sorry, that is incorrect," said Ms. Colman.

"Oh," groaned the boys in 2A. Hank looked at his feet.

"Karen? Can you spell 'gallery'?"

"Gallery. G-A-L-L-A-R-Y. Gallery."

"That is incorrect too," said Ms. Colman.

This time the girls groaned.

"The spelling bee will continue," said Ms. Colman.

Bobby let out a cheer.

Hank and Karen spelled several more words each. Then Ms. Colman said, "Karen, your next word is 'trailer.' "

"Trailer. T-R-A-I-L-O-R. Trailer."

"I am afraid that is incorrect. Hank? Can you spell 'trailer'?"

"Trailer. T-R-A-I-L-E-R. Trailer."

"Yes," said Ms. Colman. "Excellent,

Hank. You are the winner of our spelling bee."

Bobby, Chris, Omar, Ian, and Ricky cheered. They gave each other high fives. They cried, "Boys rule!"

"Karen," Ms. Colman continued, "you did a wonderful job. Both of you spelled some very difficult words. Hank, next week you will play against the winner in room two-B."

I wonder who that is, thought Hank. And just then he heard cheering coming

from Mr. Berger's room. Ms. Colman opened the door. She and Mr. Berger spoke for a few seconds. Then Ms. Colman closed the door. "The winner in two-B," she said, "is Debbie Dvorak."

"Yes!" cried Audrey.

"Girls rule!" shouted Leslie.

"You boys just wait until next week," added Hannie.

10

SATURDAY

Hank was glad the spelling bee was over. He was glad he had won, of course. But mostly he was glad it was over. His stomach felt much better. He was looking forward to Saturday.

On Saturday, Hank's father took Hank and his sisters to Burger Town for lunch. When they came home, Hank turned on his computer. He wanted to play a new mystery game. Hank was in the middle of solving a crime when he heard the doorbell ring. The next thing he heard was footsteps running up the stairs, then voices calling, "Hi, Hank!"

Hank turned around. He saw Omar,

Ricky, and Bobby run into his room. Each was carrying a small paper bag.

"Hi," Hank replied, surprised.

"We brought you some stuff," said Omar.

"More word lists?" asked Hank.

"No! Good stuff."

"Yeah," said Bobby. "We were just at the store." Bobby dumped out the bag he had been carrying. Out tumbled two candy bars, some fireballs, a baseball card, and several packages of bubble gum.

Ricky sat on the floor next to Bobby. He turned his bag upside down. Out fell a sheet of tattoos, a racing car, an eraser that looked like a monster, and a small rubber ball.

In Omar's bag were six pieces of candy, a package of crackle gum, a puzzle on a key chain, and another racing car.

Bobby gave Hank one of his candy bars and two fireballs. Ricky gave him the eraser and several tattoos. Omar gave him a piece of candy and the racing car.

"Well . . . thanks!" said Hank. "Why are you — " He had started to say, "Why are you giving me this stuff?" But that would have sounded rude. So instead he said, "You *bought* all this stuff? With your own money?" And then he thanked the boys again. Hank was impressed. He was not good about saving his allowance, so he never had much money.

"What are you doing today?" Bobby asked Hank.

"Playing computer games," Hank replied. "Want to see?"

The boys stayed for an hour, eating candy and solving mysteries.

Hank felt happy. He belonged.

11

TRAITORS

The next days passed quickly. On Sunday, Hank played computer games. On Monday, Omar and Chris shared some more candy with Hank. On Tuesday, Ricky helped Hank study some new words. And on Wednesday, Bobby asked Hank to play basketball with the other boys at recess.

The second-grade spelling bee was just two days away. Hank Reubens versus Debbie Dvorak. All the boys, even the boys in 2B, were rooting for Hank to win. And all the girls, even the girls in 2A, were rooting for Debbie to win.

"Boys rule!" the boys would shout at recess.

"No, *girls* rule!" the girls would shout back.

Thursday was the day before the big spelling bee.

"You can beat Debbie," Ricky said to Hank at recess. "You could beat her on the first word. If she goes first and she spells her word wrong and you spell it right, then you have won. You could beat her in one little minute. The world's shortest spelling bee."

"Yeah," said Hank. "Maybe." He grinned. The boys were sure he was going to win. And they were proud of him for winning the practice bees and the first spelling bee. That was a nice feeling.

When school was over, Hank hurried out of 2A. Halfway down the hall, he remembered he had left his scarf behind. It was probably in his cubby. Hank went back to his classroom. It was already empty. (Ms. Colman was talking to Mr. Berger next door.) Hank headed for the coatroom. Then he stopped. He could hear voices coming from the coatroom. Bobby and Ricky were in there.

"He has to win tomorrow," Hank heard Ricky say.

"Did you collect all the money?" Bobby asked.

"Almost. Some of the kids in Mr. Berger's room have not paid yet."

"How much money will we make if he wins this time?"

"I think about — " Ricky started to say as he walked out of the coatroom. Then he saw Hank.

Hank narrowed his eyes. "What were you talking about?" he asked.

Ricky's face grew pink. "Well . . ."

"You bet on me, didn't you? . . . Didn't you?"

"Well . . ." Ricky said again.

"Oh, we might as well tell him the truth. He will probably find out anyway," said Bobby. "Yes, we bet on you, Hank. I mean, all the *boys* in our class bet that you would win. The girls bet that Karen would win."

"Keep your voice down, Bobby," Ricky said in a loud whisper. "Ms. Colman will hear you."

Bobby lowered his voice. "Since you won, we boys got to split all the money. We got three dollars each."

"Is that where you got the money for the candy and everything?" asked Hank.

The boys nodded.

"Wasn't it nice of us to share it with you?" said Ricky.

Hank ignored him. "Is everyone betting on the next spelling bee?"

"Yup," said Bobby. "Everyone in two-A *and* two-B. Except you and Debbie. Debbie does not know about the bets."

Hank could feel his face growing hot. "So you just wanted to make money off of me," he said. "You are not really my friends."

"Um, yes we are," said Ricky, whispering. He glanced toward Mr. Berger's room. "I mean we *did* share our stuff with you."

"And you were not really being nice to

me. You were not really proud of me when I won. You were just glad *you* won the money. Well, you know what I think of you guys? I think you are traitors. All of you. Everyone in this class is a traitor!" Hank grabbed his scarf out of his cubby. Then he stomped out of room 2A.

12

LOSER

Hank was mad at everyone in his class. Even Ian. Ian had bet on him too, and he had not told Hank about the bet. He had just taken his three dollars. Hank wondered what Ian had bought with his money. Still, Hank was not as mad at Ian or the girls in his class as he was at Ricky, Bobby, Omar, and Chris. They were the ones who had told the kids to bet on Hank and Karen. The others had just gone along with their idea. (Hank realized that Karen probably did not know about the bet either.) They were the ones who had encouraged Hank to win — so *they* could win money. Worst of all, they were the ones who had *pretended* to be Hank's new friends.

Hank was so mad that he did not eat his supper that night. He was so mad that he was mean to his sisters and rude to his father. He was so mad that he could not sleep.

When Hank walked into 2A the next day, he would not speak to any of his classmates. He sat at his desk and read a book and ignored them. He even ignored Ricky when Ricky leaned in front of him and said, "Hi, Hank."

Later that morning Ms. Colman said, "Well, class, it is time for the big event. We are going to go to Mr. Berger's room for the spelling bee."

Hank's classmates sat on the floor in Mr. Berger's room. Hank and Debbie stood in front of the chalkboard. Ms. Colman gave Debbie the first word. She spelled it correctly. Then Hank took his turn, then Debbie took her second turn.

"Okay, Hank, your turn again," said

Ms. Colman. "Please spell 'mountain.' "

Mountain. That was an easy one. "Mountain," Hank repeated. "M-O-U-N-T-A-I-N." Hank paused. Then he said, "E. Mountain."

"I am sorry. That is incorrect," said Ms. Colman.

Hank looked at the kids in the room. He looked directly at Bobby, Omar, Chris, and Ricky, who were sitting together. He smiled a small smile.

"Debbie, can you spell 'mountain'?" asked Ms. Colman.

"Of course," replied Debbie. "Mountain. M-O-U-N-T-A-I-N. Mountain."

"Excellent!" said Ms. Colman. "Debbie is our second-grade winner."

"Congratulations, Debbie," added Mr. Berger. He handed her a golden trophy.

Debbie grinned. And the girls in the room cheered and clapped and cried, "Girls rule!"

All the girls are going to win a little money now, thought Hank. Bobby will probably pay them at recess. Well, good. It is better than the boys winning money.

Hank tried to feel good about what he had done, but somehow he could not. He thought about it during the rest of the morning, and during lunch. And during recess, which he spent alone. The more he thought about it, the worse he felt. He was not sure *why*, but he knew it had been wrong to lose on purpose. Besides, he had *wanted* to win. He just did not like the betting.

Recess was not quite over, but Hank went inside anyway. He hurried to 2A. Ms. Colman was sitting at her desk. She was alone in the room.

"Ms. Colman?" said Hank from the doorway. "Can I talk to you?"

"Of course," replied Ms. Colman.

Hank sat down at Karen Brewer's desk. "Well, um, see . . . I lost the spelling bee today on purpose. I know how to spell 'mountain.' I know there is no E at the end."

Ms. Colman looked thoughtful. "That did seem like an odd mistake," she replied. "Why did you want to lose the spelling bee?"

Hank thought about Omar and Bobby and the other boys. He thought about the bets. He opened his mouth. And all he said was, "I was — I guess I was tired of getting so much attention. But I wanted you to know what I did. Debbie can keep the prize, though." Hank glanced up then. He saw Omar in the doorway. He had a feeling that Omar had just overheard everything he had said.

OMAR TELLS THE TRUTH

Omar was staring at Hank. He looked surprised. And a little impressed.

Ms. Colman glanced up then, and she saw Omar too. "Omar?" she said. "Is recess over already?"

Omar nodded. He stepped into the room. The other kids trickled in behind him. Hank looked at Ms. Colman. Ms. Colman looked at Hank, then at Omar. "Omar?" she said again. "Is there something you would like to say?"

Omar drew in a deep breath. He let it out. Then he said, "Hank did not tell you the whole truth, Ms. Colman. I mean, he did not lie. He just did not tell you everything."

"What did he leave out?" asked Ms. Colman.

"He left out the part about the betting."

"The *bet*ting? What betting?"

"Well," began Omar, "the boys kept saying Hank would win the spelling bee, and the girls said Debbie would win. So Chris and Bobby and Ricky and I told all the kids to *bet* on the winner. All the boys bet on Hank and all the girls bet on Debbie." Omar paused. "We told the kids in *our* class to bet on Hank or Karen in the first spelling bee. Everyone knew about it except Hank and Karen. When Hank won, the boys each got three dollars. We would have gotten more if he had beaten Debbie. But yesterday Hank found out about the bets, and he got really mad, so — "

"So he lost on purpose," Ms. Colman finished for him.

"Yes," said Omar. He was staring down at his feet.

Ms. Colman said nothing more for a moment. Hank thought she looked angry. Even though Ms. Colman almost *never* looked angry. At last she said, "I believe I need to speak with Mr. Berger now." Ms. Colman stood up. She walked through the door to Mr. Berger's room.

Hank looked at Omar. "Wow," he said. "You told the truth."

"And you did not. You tried to protect Chris and Bobby and Ricky and me. Thanks. We did not really deserve it."

Omar looked around the room. He found the other boys and told them what Hank had done.

"Really?" said Bobby. "You tried to protect us, Hank?" Hank nodded. "Well, thanks. Thanks a lot, Hank. You are okay."

14

No Recess

Ms. Colman returned from Mr. Berger's room a few minutes later. She shut the door behind her. It was time for math, but Ms. Colman said, "Omar, Bobby, Chris, and Ricky, please see me at the back of the room. The rest of you may read your library books at your desks."

Hank watched the boys gather in the reading corner with Ms. Colman. They were right behind him. He could hear almost everything Ms. Colman said. He could not see her face, but her voice sounded serious.

"Boys," Ms. Colman began, "betting is gambling, and gambling is illegal in many places. Did you know that? That means it is against the law. Against the *law.*" Ms. Colman let that sink in. "It is definitely not a good idea," she went on. "Some people lose lots of money when they gamble or place bets. *Lots* of money. Now I know you did not know any of this when you decided to take bets on the spelling bee. However, you must have known that you were *using* Hank and Karen. And then Hank and Debbie. You did not tell them what you were doing, and you planned to make money off of them. If one of them studied hard and won, some of *you* would make money. Does that seem fair?"

"No," Hank heard the boys mumble.

"Okay," said Ms. Colman.

"Are you going to punish us?" Bobby asked Ms. Colman.

Ms. Colman sighed. "Before I figure out how to handle this matter, I must speak with Mrs. Titus."

"The *prin*cipal?" squeaked Omar.

"Yes. Mr. Berger is going to speak to

her too. But first I am going to talk to our entire class, while Mr. Berger speaks to *his* class. Before that, though, I would like you to apologize to Hank."

Hank felt a hand on his shoulder then. It was Ms. Colman. "Hank, could you turn around for a minute, please?" she said.

Hank turned around in his chair. He found himself facing the boys.

"Boys?" said Ms. Colman.

The boys were hanging their heads. "Sorry," they mumbled.

"Excuse me?" said Ms. Colman.

"We're sorry, Hank," said Chris. "Really."

"Yeah, we are really sorry," said Ricky.

"Betting on you was not nice," added Bobby.

"Neither was lying to you," said Omar. "Sorry, Hank."

"Thank you," Ms. Colman said to the boys. "Now you may return to your seats."

The boys sat down at their desks. Ms. Colman stood at the front of the room.

Next door, Mr. Berger was standing at the front of *his* room.

Ms. Colman explained to the class that betting was not a good idea and that in many places it is against the law, and that what the kids had done to Hank and Karen and Debbie was not fair and not nice. "Mr. Berger and I will talk to Mrs. Titus today and see what she has to say about this. Then we will talk to you again," added Ms. Colman.

At the end of the day, just before the fi-

nal bell rang, Ms. Colman said to her class, "Mrs. Titus has thought about the betting, and she is not pleased. She has decided that our class may not have recess for a week. Neither may Mr. Berger's." (Hank waited for his classmates to groan, but they were silent.) "Also, each of you is to give back any money you made on bets. If you have already spent it, you must earn it. Give the money to me and I will return it to the kids who first placed the bets. Mr. Berger is doing the same thing in his class.

Furthermore, Mrs. Titus is going to announce on Monday that betting is strictly forbidden at Stoneybrook Academy. All right, kids. Class is dismissed. We will have a fresh start Monday morning."

SPELLING CHAMP

On Monday morning, when Hank entered room 2A, he put a smile on his face. He was ready for a fresh start.

"Good morning, Hank," said Ms. Colman.

"Good morning," Hank replied cheerfully.

"May I speak with you for a moment, please?"

Uh-oh. Hank's smile faded. Now what?

"Hank," said Ms. Colman when he was standing by her desk. "Mr. Berger and I had a talk after school on Friday. We decided that we should have another spelling bee for you and Debbie, since you lost the last one on purpose. Maybe Debbie would have won it anyway, or maybe you would have won. We decided another bee is only fair to you and Debbie. We are going to hold it first thing this morning. Now, do not be nervous. You will do fine."

And that was how, just twenty minutes later, Hank found himself in Mr. Berger's room. He was standing next to Debbie, and his classmates were sitting on the floor, looking at him. Once again Ms. Colman gave the spelling words to Hank and Debbie.

For a very long time, neither Hank nor Debbie missed a word. Back and forth they went. The other kids in the room were quiet, listening. Finally, on the eighth word, which was *purchase*, Debbie made a mistake. But Hank could not spell the word correctly either, so the bee continued. They spelled the next six words. Then Ms. Colman said, "All right, Debbie. Deliver."

"Deliver," Debbie repeated. "D-I-L-I-V-E-R. Deliver."

"I am sorry. That is incorrect." (Hank saw the girls slump and the boys sit up straighter.) "Hank? Can you spell 'deliver'?"

"Deliver," said Hank. "D-E-L-I-V-E-R. Deliver."

Ms. Colman and Mr. Berger looked at each other. Then they smiled. Mr. Berger said, "Well, we have a winner at last. Congratulations, Hank. You are one terrific speller. You are the champ."

"Congratulations to Debbie too," added Ms. Colman. "She may have come in second, but she is also a terrific speller."

The kids in 2A and 2B began to clap their hands. And then the boys began to chant, "Boys rule, boys rule!"

Mr. Berger handed Hank a golden trophy.

"Thank you," said Hank. Then he turned to Debbie. He had to shout to be

heard. "Is this the trophy you got on Friday?" he asked.

"No. Mr. Berger let me keep it," Debbie replied. "But I did not really want it. You know what? On Friday morning, right before our first bee, I found out about the betting too. I was really mad. And then when I won, I did not know whether to feel happy or sad. I just felt kind of funny. I was really glad you told Ms. Colman the truth, Hank."

"Thank you," said Hank, even though he had told her only part of the truth.

Hank looked at his classmates then. Bobby and Ricky and Omar and Chris were chanting "Boys rule" along with the other boys. They were smiling. Hank was pretty sure they were really and truly proud of him. That was nice. He did not think they would ever be his best friends, though. But then, they never *had* been his best friends. And Hank had been fine anyway.

"Hank?" said a voice, and Hank realized he had been daydreaming. He looked down. Ian was sitting in front of him.

"Yes?" said Hank.

"I am sorry I did not tell you about the betting," said Ian. "I guess I should have. But everyone would have been mad at me. They were going to get mad at me just for *not betting.* That is why I bet on you. But I did not want to. And I hid the money I earned. I was not going to spend it. I already gave it back to Ms. Colman."

Hank grinned. He felt a lot better. "Hey," he said. "We learned the weirdest thing in the Star Club last week. I could show it to you at lunch today."

"Cool," said Ian.

Hank gave Ian a high five. Then he and Ian walked back to 2A together.

L. GODWIN

About the Author

ANN M. MARTIN lives in New York and loves animals, especially cats. She has two cats of her own, Gussie and Woody.

Other books by Ann M. Martin that you might enjoy are *Rachel Parker, Kindergarten Show-Off* and the Baby-sitters Club series. She has also written the Baby-sitters Little Sister series starring Karen Brewer, one of the kids in Ms. Colman's class.

Ann grew up in Princeton, New Jersey where she had many wonderful teachers like Ms. Colman. Ann likes ice cream, *I Love Lucy*, and especially sewing.

THE KIDS
IN
MS. COLMAN'S CLASS

A new series by Ann M. Martin

Don't miss #12

BABY ANIMAL ZOO

Going to the zoo was okay, because all the animals were in habitats. They could not get out. But this field trip sounded awful. Getting up close to mothers and babies? Touching or even holding a baby animal? Pamela would rather walk on a tightrope.

Maybe not everyone would have to touch an animal. Maybe Pamela could just watch others touch them. But she would still have to be pretty close. What if an animal broke free and jumped on her? What if one bit her?